I'll Be O.K.

RANDALL L. LANGE, DVM
Illustrated by Betsy Tarpley Lesher

JoshCo, LLC • Knoxville, Tennessee

PUBLISHER'S ACKNOWLEDGEMENT

The publisher wishes to acknowledge the efforts of many individuals who helped to make this project a reality. Special thanks to John Payne of Bayer's animal health group for his vision of the importance of the human and animal bond; to Scott Burt of Children's Miracle Network for his commitment to this project; to Teresa Goddard for her never-ending dedication to seeing this project completed; and to Jennifer Sifton for her ability to coordinate all of the partners' efforts. Watch for future adventures of Josh and Friends™ in the months ahead.

I'll Be O.K.

Published by: JoshCo,LLC
P.O. Box 23815
Knoxville, Tennessee 37923-1815

Illustration: Betsy Tarpley Lesher

Art Direction/Design: Sally Tarpley Nelson

Editing: Linda Blake

Library of Congress Catalog Number: 99-60480

ISBN: 0-9668355-0-6

Manufactured in the United States of America

First Printing 1999

10 9 8 7 6 5 4 3

Dedicated
with love to
my twin, Dr. Rick,
my dad, Frank Lange,
and
to Mom Champion.

I know you are all O.K.

MY FAMILY

JOSH

Hi! My name is Josh, and I'm a Golden Retriever. You know, blond and loving with a tail that just won't stop wagging! I'm one year old, about seven or eight in human years. I live with my family--Jessica, my best friend, and her Mom and Dad. We all love each other very much! I also have a dog buddy named Smudge. She shares my rug at night and tries to keep me out of trouble!

We Golden Retriever puppies are famous for having adventures.

One day when my family left Smudge and me in the house, I proved that I was a great chewer--uh, retriever. (By the way, we Goldens are called retrievers because we like to retrieve--go get--things.) Anyway, I pushed open Jessica's mom's closet door and chewed--uh, retrieved-- seven different shoes! After playing in the shoes, I saw something on the shelves waaaayyyy up above me.

And since we Goldens are also known for being curious, I started tugging at some dresses when--Blam!!! "Who turned out the lights?" I barked.

Suddenly, I was buried underneath a pile of lacy things that smelled like--Sniff, Sniff--perfume? Oh no! guess what? They were Jessica's mom's underwear!!!!!

Panicking, I thought, "I gotta get out of here before Smudge sees me wearing these undies!" I ran out of the closet with one wrapped around my hind leg and another with straps over my shoulder. Romping down the hallway and the steps, I saw Jessica's mom. I barked, "Oh, Hi! Welcome back! What? Oh, these undies? Why, they must have jumped on me as I was snoozing!"

Since then, I have spent most of my time in the backyard chasing rabbits and digging wayyyyy down in our flower beds. Burying my nose, sniffing and snorting, I'm in dog heaven, especially when it's muddy and I look like I've been dipped in chocolate. But when I run into the house to show my family my chocolate coat, they march me out into the yard, grab shampoo and a hose, and--you guessed it--bath time! Oh, what adventures I have!

Speaking of adventures, let me tell you about my most exciting one. Not long ago, Jessica and her parents took me to visit Dr. Rick for a check up. (I guess Jessica could tell that my tummy had been hurting for awhile.) When we walked into his hospital, I smelled a super-clean smell. Also, without a doubt--no question--I smelled CATS! And..........RABBITS!!!! I barked, "Where are they? Let me at those fuzzy little hair balls!" In the meantime, a nice lady came over, patted me on the head, and told me I'd gotten more handsome since my last visit. Then she took us into a small room and left.

I could hear other dogs nearby.

There was a poodle that barked in French.

There was a basset hound that sounded like a fog horn.

And a chihuahua with a Mexican accent!

Finally, Dr. Rick came in, patted me on the head, and told me how I'd grown. (All that good food and exercise paid off!) When Dr. Rick and his helper set me on the examining table, I was so nervous I messed on it.

How embarassing! Then Dr. Rick pressed against my chest with a shiny round thing that had two tubes. (He called it a stetho---What?) Brrrr! I shivered! Moving it all over my chest, he asked me to breathe deep--in and out, out and in, in and out. I felt silly--but it didn't hurt!

Next Dr. Rick looked inside my ears with a teeny light that kinda tickled. Then he moved his fingers all over my body, pushing in here, then there, watching my eyes and listening to see if I hurt. I squinted and moaned when he pushed on my tummy. It was sore and had hurt for days, especially after I ate. Looking into my eyes, he nodded and smiled. Feeling warm inside, I wagged my tail; and he smiled again.

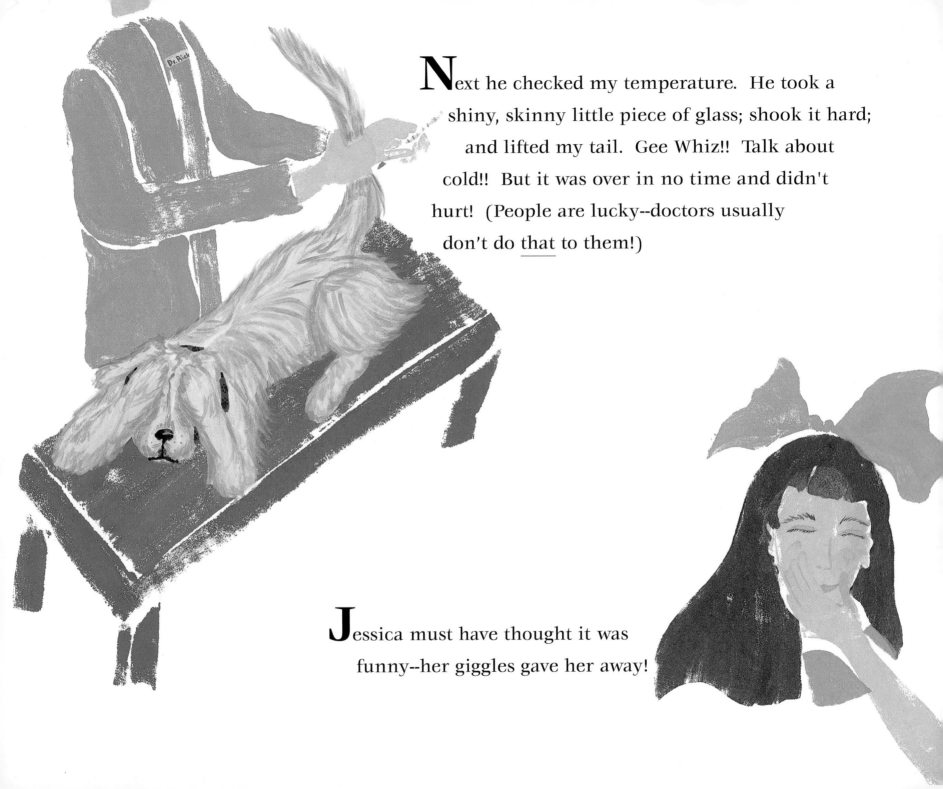

Next he checked my temperature. He took a shiny, skinny little piece of glass; shook it hard; and lifted my tail. Gee Whiz!! Talk about cold!! But it was over in no time and didn't hurt! (People are lucky--doctors usually don't do <u>that</u> to them!)

Jessica must have thought it was funny--her giggles gave her away!

Suddenly the room got very dark, like at bedtime--no moon, no stars, nothing. The next person I saw was Dr. Rick looking into my eyes with a bright light. His face was so close to mine I could feel his breath. A little scared, I felt like crying.

But Jessica hugged me and said, "Don't worry, Josh. I love you, and everything will be fine." And then I knew that I'd be O.K........

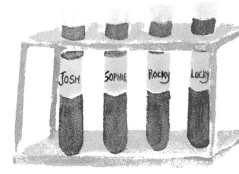

When Dr. Rick said he needed to stick my arm with a needle, I thought, "You gotta be kidding!" But, in a kind and gentle way, he explained he needed to look at my blood to see why I hurt. When Dr. Rick asked me which arm I wanted him to stick, I told him my left because I <u>always</u> shake with my right! He also told me I could either look at Jessica when he took my blood sample, or bark my favorite song, "You Ain't Nothin' But A Hound Dog!" When Dr. Rick stuck me, I closed my eyes <u>real</u> tight, held <u>real</u> still, and cried--just a little.

And he said sometimes you can blow the hurt away--
"Jessica, would you blow on my arm, please?"
I barked. A few seconds later, I saw my
blood running into a little tube.
Dr. Rick put a band-aid on my arm
and gave me a treat for being
so good. Yummm!!

Then Dr. Rick left the room. I could hear him outside talking about me in really long words. But Jessica and her parents kept hugging and petting me. When Dr. Rick came back and said I needed more tests, I got kinda scared. Jessica turned away, wiped her eyes, and looked scared, too. I just wanted to go home, play in the yard, chase some rabbits, and dig up some flowers. I guess Jessica understood how I felt because she smiled, patted me on the head and said, "It'll be O.K. You go with Dr. Rick. Mom and Dad and I will be waiting for you. We promise!" So, even though I was really scared, I knew I'd be O.K.!

Next we went into another room. Dr. Rick and his helper, wearing funny looking gowns and gloves, laid me on a table. I barked, "Brrrr! It's cold! And slippery! What's going on?" As Dr. Rick talked softly to me and stroked my neck, I relaxed a little. I thought, "I guess I can trust you, can't I?"

I was on the table hooked up to a machine that had flashing lights and went "hummmm" and "whirrrr" and "ding." Dr. Rick held me still while a light went over me. Even though I was scared, I knew that Jessica and her parents were nearby. Dr. Rick smiled and stroked me again. And guess what? I didn't feel a thing! Then I knew I'd be O.K.

Later Dr. Rick walked me to Jessica and her parents, who were waiting just as they promised. I was so happy to see them my tummy hurt just a little bit less. I barked, "Wait until I tell you about my adventure!"

In a few minutes, Dr. Rick took us to a special room. He showed Jessica and her parents black pictures held up to a box with sunlight in it. Dr. Rick kept pointing to a spot on one of the pictures. I couldn't understand what he was saying; but whenever I heard my name, I'd just wag my tail! By then Jessica and her parents seemed to have something in their eyes.......Dr. Rick said I needed to come back the next day for an operation. He told me I'd be asleep and wouldn't feel a thing. As we left, the nice lady up front gave me a treat. Then we went home to get ready for the next part of my adventure.

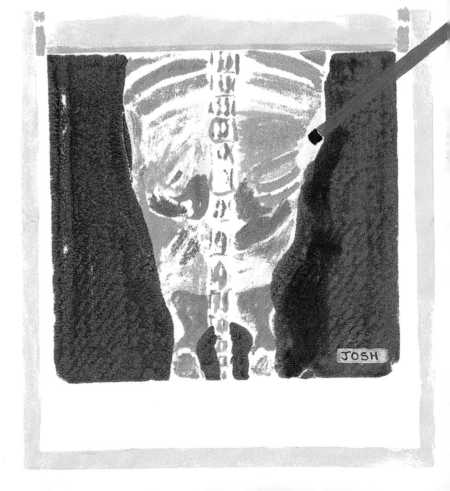

That night Jessica told me I couldn't have anything to eat or drink after 8 o'clock--not even popcorn or dog biscuits! And then no breakfast in the morning. By midnight, my tummy growled like--like a dog!

Early the next morning, we drove back to the hospital. As Jessica turned to leave me with Dr. Rick, I screamed, "Jessica, don't leave!!" Spinning back around, she squeezed my neck, gave me a big hug, and told me she loved me. And even though I was scared, I knew once again that I'd be O.K.!

Dr. Rick walked me into a room and gave me a shot he called a "little pinch." "Hey, whatcha doin'?!" I yelped. Before long, I was feeling kinda dizzy.

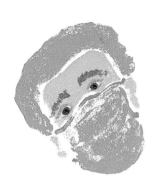
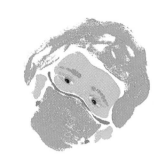

Dr. Rick and his helper looked silly floating around in their masks and caps! As his helper began shaving my tummy, my beautiful golden hair fell to the floor. I wondered if the other dogs would laugh at me, but Dr. Rick told me that soon my hair would grow back--maybe thicker and more golden than before! Then he scrubbed my tummy with orange-looking stuff that kinda tickled! I wondered if my tummy would always look like a pumpkin!

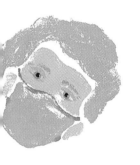

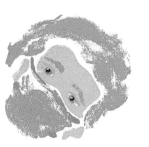

Next they rolled me into the operating room. Dr. Rick told me to start counting bunnies backward from 100. I began, "100 bunnies." Then over the top of my nose he put a black cone hooked to a hose. Sniff, Sniff--it smelled funny, kinda sweet and burned my nose a little. I'd never smelled that smell before. It sure wasn't a BUNNY smell! I continued counting, "99 bunnies, 98 bunnies." As I relaxed, "97 bunnies. Boy, my eyelids seem heavy........ 96 bunnies, 95 bunnies........." I felt like I was floating--so peaceful, so quiet. "94 bunnies........" Then I thought, "How come there aren't any stars out tonight? And where's the moon? How can I howl at it when it's nowhere to be seen? This might be heaven! Guess I'll just rest now........so quiet........so peaceful........I feel really light, like I could float away........I'll be O.K........."

T he next thing I knew my throat felt funny--so dry--like I couldn't swallow. And my stomach felt a little topsy-turvy. Then I listened, "I can hear something. Shhhh! It sounds like Jessica! What's that light? It's kinda swirly. Dr. Rick? Please stand still so I can see you! Hey, where'd the bunnies go? Jessica! You missed my wild adventure! Scratch my chin, please........ Ooh, that feels good. If I were a cat, I'd purr!"

I had to let them know that I was O.K. I barked, "Come on tail, how come you won't wag? How else can I tell them I'm O.K.? Come on, just a teensy-weensy wag will do! It worked just fine this morning. Commmmmme on!" Suddenly, the tip moved. I barked louder, "Somebody take a look-- IT'S WAGGING!!!! Thank you thank you thank you thank you! See Jessica, I'm O.K.!!!!"

Then I thought, "Wait a minute! What's that clear little hose running into my leg? Maybe I'll chew on it! On second thought, I'd better not! After all, Jessica still hasn't forgotten when 'guess who' chewed up her favorite Sunday school shoes. I'll leave the hose for now. It keeps dripping........dripping........Hmmm........I'm still thirsty.......My tummy feels tight and cold. It itches and is kinda red. Hey, what are those little strings coming out of my skin? They look like shoestrings, pulled up real tight!"

I looked around. The room was spinning.
Every time I lifted my head, boom!! I crash landed.
Sleepily I thought, "I'm so tired........and I can still
smell that sweet smell. Guess I'll take........another........
short........nap........Hmmmmmm............"

When I woke up again, I felt better, and the room
wasn't spinning. I barked, "Is anybody here? Ooh!
Keep rubbing my ears, will you? Jessica, is that you?........
Oh, I love you love you love you love you love you!!!!
See my tail wagging?!!!   And here comes Dr. Rick
with a big smile on his face."

Dr. Rick

Dr. Rick said the operation went just fine and I could go home the next day. He told me my tummy might be sore for a few days, and I should definitely not chase my buddy, Smudge. "That's O.K.," I thought, "I can always chase her next week!"

Later that night, I tried to get up. Boy I hurt!........ And I cried........ I began barking, "Hey, can anybody hear me? I'm kinda thirsty........ Who is that nice lady in white? Will you help me?........ Sure, I'll take a drink. How about a snack? Would you please tuck my blanket in for me? (Boy, training humans sure is tough!) How about getting my favorite toy? The stuffed bunny........but don't tell!!!" When I finally went to sleep that night, I dreamed of being at home on my rug with Smudge snuggled up beside me.

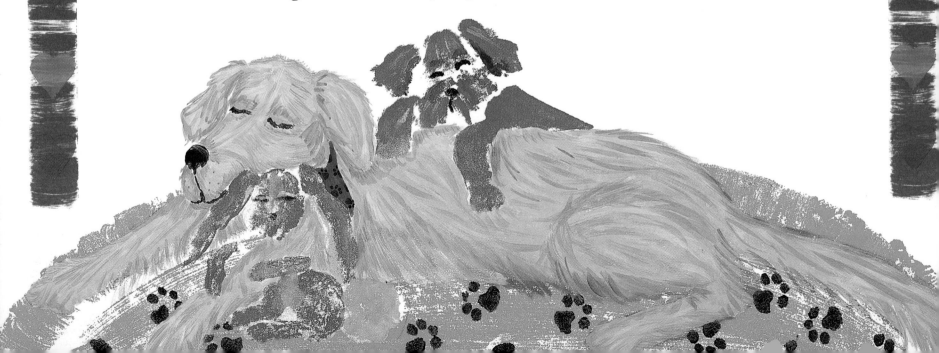

The next day, Jessica and her parents drove me home. Thinking back, I see my time at Dr. Rick's hospital <u>was</u> an adventure! At first, I wasn't sure I trusted Dr. Rick, but now I know he helped me feel better. Sure, I was scared; but it wasn't so bad. After all, I got some get-well treats from my family and friends.

Plus, I've never been petted and hugged so much. With my family and Dr. Rick and his helpers caring for me, I knew........
you remember don't you?........ I knew all along that I'd be O.K.!!!! And I was. I <u>was</u> O.K.!!!

And now I'm here for you--any time, any place. Whenever you need me, just give me a hug or squeeze; and I promise I'll love you--Forever!!! Remember, I know what it's like to visit a doctor and a hospital. And I've been through some of the tests and treatment you might have. So take me with you when you go to the doctor or hospital. I'll always be by your side, waiting for you to give me a big hug and a squeeze.

Come on! Lets go see your doctor
and find out when you begin <u>your</u>
adventure in feeling better. Remember,
I'll be with you--Always. And with
everybody's love and help,
<u>you'll be O.K</u>.........
just like me!

THE AUTHOR

Dr. Randall L. Lange is a graduate of Iowa State University with a Doctorate of Veterinary Medicine. He has practiced small-animal medicine and surgery for twenty-four years and is currently in practice with his twin brother, Dr. Rick.
In addition to his practice of veterinary medicine and his writing, Dr. Lange is a past chair of the public relations committee for the Tennessee Veterinary Medical Association. He has also volunteered as a youth Sunday school teacher and coach for both youth soccer and basketball. He lives in Knoxville, Tennessee with his wife, daughter, and their Golden Retriever, the real "Josh".

THE ILLUSTRATOR

Betsy Tarpley Lesher is an artist who works in several media--including clay, acrylic paint and salt dough--as well as enjoying jewelry making and accent furniture decorating. Her unique style of illustration for the book uses a stamp method with overpainting to achieve a fresh, upbeat look which reflects the story's positive outlook of a serious subject. A graduate of the University of Tennessee, she lives in Knoxville Tennessee with her husband, two daughters, and Australian Shepherd, "Sophie".